and the
UNUSUAL YAK

For Salome
J.S.

For Michael & Ben
C.E.

Reading Consultant: Prue Goodwin, Lecturer in literacy and children's books

ORCHARD BOOKS
338 Euston Road, London NW1 3BH
Orchard Books Australia
Level 17/207 Kent Street, Sydney, NSW 2000

First published in 2012
First paperback publication in 2013

ISBN 978 1 40831 332 9 (hardback)
ISBN 978 1 40831 340 4 (paperback)

A CIP catalogue record for this book is available from the British Library.

1 3 5 7 9 10 8 6 4 2 (hardback)
1 3 5 7 9 10 8 6 4 2 (paperback)

Printed in China

Orchard Books is a division of Hachette Children's Books,
an Hachette UK company.
www.hachette.co.uk

ZAK ZOO

and the
UNUSUAL YAK

Justine Smith • Clare Elsom

ORCHARD

Zak Zoo lives at Number One, Africa Avenue.
His mum and dad are away on
safari, so his animal family is looking
after him. Sometimes things get a little . . .

. . . WILD!

Emily

Pam

Dad

Mum

Zak

Nanny
Hilda

Bob

Tom

Charlie

Mia (Zak's best friend)

Ping

Late one night, Tom the post-bird
delivered a letter to Zak Zoo.

Little green tent
The Snowfields
Siberia

Dear Zak,

We have sent you an unusual
yak. He will arrive on Friday.
Please take special care
of him.
Love,
Mum and Dad

P.S. Are you eating your
greens?

On Friday, Zak's best friend Mia
came for breakfast.
"There is a big crate in your
garden," she said.
"That will be my yak!" said Zak.

Zak and Mia went to look at the crate. It jumped and bumped. "He's a very lively yak," said Zak.

Inside the crate, the yak moaned and groaned.

"He's not a very happy yak," said Mia.

The yak went quiet.

"Perhaps he's asleep," said Zak.

"Let's get him out," said Zak, and he went to get his tools.

Zak opened up the crate.

"Hello, Mr Yak," he said politely.

The yak didn't reply.

Zak thought the yak might be hungry after his long journey. So he took him into the kitchen for a snack.

After his snack, the yak went to lie down on the sofa. His shaggy coat dropped hair everywhere.

He was very messy and VERY

smelly!

Next, the yak went to look upstairs,
leaving dirty hoof-prints everywhere.
He seemed happy with his new home.

The yak did an awful lot of
unusual things.

That night he sang to the moon.

The yak really was unusually rude. He never said "please" or "thank you".

He liked to sit in front of the open fridge, and he never helped with the washing up.

He liked to take cold baths.

He liked to make milkshakes with
ice cream.

Poor Nanny Hilda spent all her
time cleaning up!

Zak wrote to his parents.

Dear Mum and Dad,

The yak has arrived safely. He is unusual, all right!
I am doing my best to take care of him.

Love,

Zak

P.S. Don't worry. I ate a green bean last week.

Zak wondered how he could take better care of the yak. He searched the internet and found out that yaks live in snowy places.

"I think this yak is too hot," said Zak.

"I think you're right," said Mia.

It was obvious that the yak needed to cool down.

"I know just what to do,"
said Zak.

He drew a picture of his idea.

Zak got to work outside, building
a new, cool house for the yak.
The yak didn't say "thank you".
He was far too rude for that.

The yak moved into his new
house, but he was still too hot.

Zak went to bed worried. But that night a strong wind blew through the tree outside his window. It gave him another idea.

He jumped out of bed and started

work at once.

Zak rebuilt the yak's house high
in the tree, where it was cool and
breezy. And then something
very unusual happened.

"Thank you," said the yak.

Written by Justine Smith • Illustrated by Clare Elsom

All priced at £4.99

Orchard Books are available from all good bookshops,
or can be ordered from our website: www.orchardbooks.co.uk,
or telephone 01235 827702, or fax 01235 827703.

Prices and availability are subject to change.